MAGGIE AND THE FEROCIOUS BEAST

THE BiG CARROT

Betty Paraskevas

Michael Paraskevas

Simon & Schuster Books for Young Readers
New York   London   Toronto   Sydney   Singapore

MAGGIE, Hamilton Hocks, and the Ferocious Beast were bird-watching in Nowhere Land when they came upon a rabbit trying to dig up a gigantic carrot.

"Hello, Mr. Rabbit," Maggie called. "It looks like you could use some help."

"This is *my* carrot," they heard him shout. "*I'll* dig it up and *I'll* get it out."

"My, my," whispered Hamilton. "What an unpleasant little fellow."

"You'll never dig up that carrot by yourself," said the Beast.

But the rabbit got madder than a speckled red hen. "I've said it before and I'll say it again:

This is *my* carrot and without a doubt, *I'll* dig it up and *I'll* get it out."

And he dug even faster.

"Maggie," murmured Hamilton, "the poor fellow looks a bit pooped."

The rabbit continued to dig until his ears went limp and his whiskers drooped. Then he slid down the handle of his shovel and landed on a pile of dirt.

"Let's carry him to that tree," said Maggie.

"He's exhausted," Hamilton remarked. "I'll fix him something to eat."

Maggie brushed the little rabbit's ears away from his eyes and patted his furry cheeks. "What's your name?" she asked.

"Nedley," he replied.

Hamilton served a pot of lettuce tea and a platter of cucumber sandwiches. They watched Nedley nibble and sip.

"Those sandwiches look delicious," remarked the Beast, his eyes fixed on the platter.

"Forget it, Beast," snapped Hamilton. "We have work to do."

"Oh, all right," said the Beast, stamping his feet as he followed Hamilton. "But I've never tasted cucumber sandwiches."

Hamilton studied the carrot. "I'll tie this rope around the top, then we'll all pull. Beast, you take the ends between your teeth. Ready? One, two, three, go!"

They pulled and pulled. The carrot didn't
budge. They tried again.
  The earth trembled. Then came the sound
of rumbling thunder as the gigantic carrot
rose from the ground—and fell with
a tremendous thud.

Nedley hobbled over. "It's mine," he gasped, "all mine."

They watched as he closed his eyes, opened his mouth wide, and bit off the tip of the carrot. He nibbled and tasted; he nibbled and tasted again.

"Oh," groaned Nedley. "I've never tasted anything so awful. I guess it's been growing in the ground so long, it tastes just like wood."

At first Maggie, the Beast, and Hamilton were silent. Then like a pot of soup that begins to boil, their bubbles of laughter exploded one by one, faster and faster.

The little fellow shook his fist and stamped his foot. "What is so funny?" he demanded.

"You," they shouted.

Nedley's anger slowly melted away, and he laughed until the tears rolled down his cheeks.

"Oh, oh," he puffed, "I really was ridiculous, wasn't I? I wasted three days trying to dig up that worthless carrot."

"Now, what are we going to do with it? We can't just leave it here," declared Hamilton.

They thought and thought. Then Maggie said, "Come closer. I have a plan."

"Oh, Maggie," cried the Beast, "that was a wonderful plan."

Hamilton announced, "Thank you, Nedley, for helping us."

"You helped me, and it was only fair that I should help you," Nedley replied.

"I'm happy with the way this story ends:
I dug up a carrot with the help of my friends.
And when you think of me, remember these words:
Nedley's carrot was fit for the birds."

SIMON & SCHUSTER BOOKS FOR YOUNG READERS
An imprint of Simon & Schuster Children's Publishing Division
1230 Avenue of the Americas, New York, New York 10020

Book design by Jennifer Reyes
The text of this book is set in 18-point Myriad Bold.
The illustrations are rendered in acrylic on paper.
Printed in Hong Kong
10 9 8 7 6 5 4 3 2 1
Library of Congress Cataloging-in-Publication Data
Paraskevas, Betty.
Maggie and the Ferocious Beast : the big carrot / Betty Paraskevas ;
illustrated by Michael Paraskevas.
p.   cm.
Summary: Maggie, Hamilton, and the Ferocious Beast help a
stubborn rabbit dig up a gigantic carrot.
ISBN 0-689-82490-4
[1. Rabbits Fiction. 2. Monsters Fiction. 3. Helpfulness Fiction.]
 I. Paraskevas, Michael, 1961- ill. II. Title.
PZ7.P2135Mag 2000
[E]—dc21
99-39432
CIP

first
edition

To Brown Johnson
for your wisdom and support